The Three BULLY Goats

Leslie Kimmelman   Illustrated by Will Terry

Albert Whitman & Company, Chicago, Illinois

To the fantastic students and staff of WECS.—L.K.

For Jocelyn, Kallie, and McKade.—W.T.

Library of Congress Cataloging-in-Publication Data

Kimmelman, Leslie.
The three bully goats / by Leslie Kimmelman ; illustrated by Will Terry.
p. cm.
Summary: Billy goat brothers Gruff, Ruff, and Tuff are bullies who rule their meadow,
but when they cross Little Ogre's bridge and are mean to the baby animals on the
other side, they are in for a surprise.
ISBN 978-0-8075-7900-8
[1. Bullies—Fiction. 2. Goats—Fiction. 3. Ghouls and ogres—Fiction.
4. Meadow animals—Fiction. 5. Animals—Infancy—Fiction.]
I. Terry, Will, 1966- ill. II. Title.
PZ7.K56493Thr 2011 [E]—dc22 2010024274

The design is by Carol Gildar.

For more information about Albert Whitman & Company,
please visit our web site at www.albertwhitman.com.

Once upon a time, there were three bully goats, Gruff, Ruff, and Tuff.

They had a good thing going, grazing day after day
in a big grassy meadow next to a rushing river.

They were such big bully goats that no one dared come too near, even though there was plenty of meadow to share. "We don't share," Tuff growled at the other animals.

So, everything was cool, except . . . the three bully goats weren't happy.

"The other side of the river looks better,"
complained Gruff. "The meadow's even grassier."

"But how do we get there?" asked Ruff. "There's an ogre guarding that creaky old bridge."

"Just one ogre?" scoffed Tuff. "Big deal. We're the three bully goats, Gruff, Ruff, and Tuff! We can take on one puny ogre."

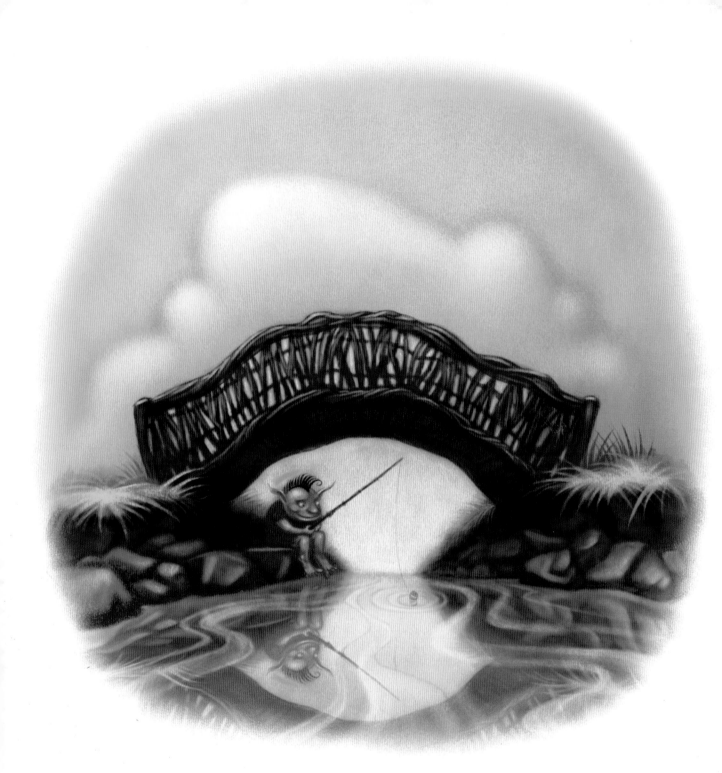

Now, the ogre that lived under the bridge *was* kind of puny. But he was cute, too, and really nice. He was friends with everybody. That is, until . . .

Trip trap trip trap trip trap. The smallest bully goat tossed his head and started across the river.

"Who's that coming across my bridge?" the ogre asked cheerfully.

"It is I, Bully Goat Gruff," answered Gruff. "Who's asking?"

Oh, no! Little Ogre had heard about the bully goats. His ears quivered, and his feet trembled, and he pulled on a purple curl. Even the youngest of those three bully goats looked big . . . and mean . . . and scary.

"Keep going, please keep going," Little Ogre whispered, crossing his warty green fingers. But no such luck. Exactly in the middle of the bridge, he heard the hoofsteps stop.

The smallest bully goat stuck his face right down under the bridge. "*You're* the ogre?" he jeered. "Ha ha ha!"

"I'm Gruff, and I mean, I'm **really** gruff.
And you, you're just a powder puff.
Now stop squawking, or I'll butt you
from here to Brazil!"

Trip trap trip trap trip trap. The bully goat continued across the bridge. Little Ogre didn't even get a chance to tell him not to trample the wildflowers and to watch out for the baby animals.

Sure enough, the smallest bully goat wasted no time trampling the sweet grass and chewing up the buttercups. Then he butted a couple of baby bunnies out of his way.

Meanwhile, *TRIP TRAP TRIP TRAP TRIP TRAP*, the medium-sized bully goat trotted across the bridge. He looked bigger than his brother, and scarier, and way meaner.

Little Ogre took a deep breath. "Who's that coming across my bridge?" he asked.

"Who wants to know?" snarled Ruff.

"I'm j-j-just asking," stuttered Little Ogre, "b-because I'd like to be f-friends."

"F-friends? Ha ha ha!" said the medium-sized bully goat.

*"I'm Ruff, and I mean, I'm **really** rough.*
And you, you're just a powder puff.
Now stop squawking, or I'll butt you
from here to Brazil!"

And *TRIP TRAP TRIP TRAP TRIP TRAP,* the bully goat crossed the bridge to the meadow on the other side.

"Careful with the wildflowers and the baby animals," Little Ogre called after him softly. But Ruff wasted no time trampling the sweet grass and chewing up the daisies. Then he butted two baby deer out of his way and went to join his brother.

TRIP TRAP TRIP TRAP TRIP TRAP. The third bully goat headed straight for the bridge. He was the biggest, scariest, and sure looked like he was the meanest of the three brothers. He was so big that the bridge swayed and groaned under his hooves.

"Who's that coming across my bridge?" squeaked out Little Ogre, trying not to faint.

"What do you mean, *your* bridge?" the third bully goat answered, then added,

> "I'm Tuff, and I mean, I'm **really** tough.
> And you, you're just a powder puff.
> Now stop squawking, or I'll butt you
>   from here to Brazil!"

With a rude and haughty toss of his head, ***TRIP TRAP TRIP TRAP TRIP TRAP,*** off went Tuff in a huff.

Little Ogre began to cry. He had tried being friendly. He had tried being polite. Nothing had worked with those bully goats. "Gruff, Ruff, and Tuff, I've had enough," he said aloud.

He thought and thought. "But what can one little ogre do?"

Scritch scratch scritch scratch, went his fingers.

Tip tap tip tap, went his toes.

Then *snip snap snip snap!* He snapped his warty finger and thumb. "I've got it!"

Little Ogre splashed over to the far side of the bridge and called loudly after the third bully goat, "Yoohoo, Tuff! The tallest grass is usually the tastiest!"

Little Ogre had remembered something. There were *some* baby animals in the tall grass who didn't need his protection at all.

Sure enough, the third bully goat wasted no time prancing straight to the tallest grasses in the meadow, uprooting wildflowers as he went. Suddenly he spotted four furry baby skunks and stopped short, a gleam in his eyes. He butted one, two, three, four skunks, head over paws, sending them tumbling across the grass.

"Oh, I'm *bad!*" he exclaimed, then called, "Hey, Gruff, Ruff! Come over here!"

As Gruff and Ruff ran up to join their brother, the third bully goat chanted:

*"I'm Tuff, and I mean, I'm **really** tough.*
And you all, you're just balls of fluff.
Now stop—"

Before he could finish his song, the little skunks brushed themselves off and squealed, "Should we use our stuff?" They turned their backsides to the three goats, raised their tails, and . . .

A-A-I-I-I-G-H-H-H!!!!!!

What a smell! What a stench! What a way to pay those bullies back!

The little skunks laughed their stinky heads off. And all the animals of the meadow joined in, laughing and chanting:

"Hip hip hooray!
We called their bluff!
So long, bully goats
Gruff, Ruff, and Tuff!"

And the three smelly bully goats? They were *so* embarrassed. They galloped *maaaaaadly* out of the meadow, across the bridge, *trip* TRIP **TRIP** *trap* TRAP **TRAP,** and far, far away—maybe as far as Brazil!— never to bully anyone again.